THE UNEXPECTED GRANDCHILDREN

JANE FLORY

Pictures by CAROLYN CROLL

Houghton Mifflin Company Boston 1977

Library of Congress Cataloging in Publication Data

Flory, Jane, 1917-
    The unexpected grandchildren.

    SUMMARY: Mr. and Mrs. Newton's life was orderly
and precise until the day they received a letter
announcing the arrival of unexpected grandchildren.
    I. Croll, Carolyn. II. Title.
PZ7.F665Un   [E]   77-5085
ISBN 0-395-25797-2

For my grandson, David John Farmer,
a book of his very own.

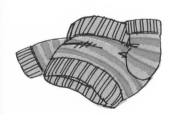

3

Halfway down the block at 1814 Beech Avenue lived Mr. and Mrs. Newton. She was short and round and tidy and he was tall and thin and careful. Their house was neat as a pin, not so much as a shoe out of place. Their meals were always on time, without fail, and neither of them ever whined or nagged or spilled their milk at the table.

No crabgrass or dandelions dared poke their heads up on the Newtons' perfect lawn. Neighbor children knew better than to step off the walk and onto the grass. When they did, Mr. Newton scolded them.

At Halloween, the children skipped 1814 Beech Avenue. They were not sure they would be welcome if they came trick-or-treating. The Newtons wondered why, but they didn't really mind if they were skipped. They didn't know much about children, but they did know that children are apt to muss up a house and wrinkle the sofa cushions and spill things. It was very important to the Newtons that nothing be mussed or wrinkled or spilled.

They liked everything to be just so. Mrs. Newton knew exactly how Mr. Newton was going to clear his throat each time he sat down to read the newspaper. Mr. Newton knew exactly how the heels of Mrs. Newton's shoes would click as she bustled around the house. And they both knew that the third step would creak when they went upstairs to bed.

They kept busy all day long. Mrs. Newton knitted and sewed and baked. She knitted sweaters and scarves and mittens for Mr. Newton. She even knitted a sweater for their well-behaved big black and white cat, Seth.

Mr. Newton kept busy in other ways. He built things. He made a tall clock carved like a tree in the forest with a little bird that flew out and said cuckoo every hour. He made it all himself and it kept perfect time.

Every day was the same as the day before. Everything about the Newtons' lives was as perfect as it could be. The clock went tick-tock, tick-tock, in the quiet house, the little bird said cuckoo, and that was all until the next hour.

But then Mrs. Newton began to look less round and cozy. She had a pale lonely look that worried Mr. Newton. "There is something wrong," he thought, "but what can it be?"

One day the mailman brought the Newtons a letter. Mrs. Newton tore it open in a hurry, for they got very few letters.

SURPRISE! it said in rather wobbly printing. ONE OF THESE DAYS SOON YOU ARE GOING TO GET A SURPRISE! THERE WILL BE A KNOCK AT THE DOOR AND WHEN YOU OPEN IT, THERE WE WILL BE, ALL OF US!

LOVE AND KISSES,
YOUR UNEXPECTED GRANDCHILDREN

Mrs. Newton's hands were trembling so she could hardly hold the paper. She called her husband and he read it, too. They did not understand it. "How can this be?" asked Mrs. Newton. "We have never had any children. How could we have grandchildren? Someone is playing a joke on us."

Mr. Newton said, "It's not a funny joke. When they knock we just won't answer the door."

They put the letter on the hall table. A little later Mrs. Newton said, "If we peeked out and they looked like nice children, I don't think it would hurt to answer the door."

"Children make a lot of noise and mess," he said, and that was that.

The next morning Mrs. Newton got out her mixing bowl.

"What are we going to have?" he asked.

"Just some cookies. Just in case." He noticed that she had lost some of her lonely look, and he was pleased.

The days went by, and they listened constantly for the knock. Day after day they waited eagerly and then anxiously and then frantically. No one came. Finally Mr. Newton said, "Perhaps we read the letter wrong. Perhaps the date was written somewhere."

They read it again. No date. Only SOON.

"On the envelope, maybe?"

He looked at the envelope a long, long time.

"Wife," he said. "We have made a terrible mistake. This letter was intended for Mr. and Mrs. Nutley of 1814 Birch Avenue. The grandchildren are not for us."

It was terribly quiet in the little house. The clock went tick-tock, tick-tock, and the cuckoo called three times. Mrs. Newton grew paler and Mr. Newton grew more worried.

"There must be something I can do," he said over and over. "There must be something I can do."

Then one afternoon an idea came to him. He put on his sweater and hurried out the door. It was almost five when he reached the newspaper office.

"Have I still time to put a want ad in your paper?" he asked the editor of the *Times Chronicle*.

"If you hurry," said the editor. "The paper goes to press at five."

There was no time to plan it carefully. He scribbled, "Wanted: Grandchildren to borrow. Any size, age, color or shape. Please come to 1814 Beech Avenue on Saturday morning at nine."

There were only five days until Saturday and they had to hurry. They made toys and baked some more cookies. She mixed the dough and he licked the bowl. She held the wood while he hammered the nails. Once in a while each one thought, "Suppose no one comes?" but neither said it out loud.

And then it was Saturday. Just as breakfast was over and the kitchen tidied, the cuckoo called nine times. They waited, but there was no knock at the door. Tick-tock, tick-tock, no knock, no knock. No one came.

They waited all morning. It was terrible. They had worked so hard and hoped so hard and no one came.

Mrs. Newton could hardly hold back her tears. Finally she said, "Well, I might as well start lunch." She went to the kitchen and Mr. Newton went out into the front yard. He leaned on the gate and looked out.

A little boy came pedaling by on his tricycle. He looked up at Mr. Newton. Mr. Newton said, "Hi there. What's your name?" The boy pedaled to the end of the block. On the way back he went slower and said, "Davey." The third time he pedaled very slowly and came to a stop at the gate.

"How come you said 'Hi'?" he asked.

"What should I say?"

"Get off my grass is what you always say."

"Well, this time I'm saying, 'Hi, Davey.' And you know what? Your bike has a squeaky wheel."

"I know, but I don't have any oil."

"Wait right there," said Mr. Newton. In a moment he was back with his oil can. While he was oiling the wheel, Davey said, "My mom saw in the paper that you wanted some kids to visit. She says nobody in his right mind would advertise for kids when they could have peace and quiet instead."

"Not us! Not anymore!" said Mr. Newton. "We've got too much peace and quiet. We need a change!"

"We yell a lot," said Davey, "and we run around a lot."

"Davey, Mrs. Newton and I would like you to visit us. We've never known any children. Tell your sisters and brothers and all your friends."

"You mean it?" asked Davey, not quite sure.

"I really mean it!"

"Well," said Davey, "you did say 'Hi.' I'll tell 'em. I'll ride all over. I'm a very fast rider."

Almost before they knew it, there was a knock at the front door. There were seven of them. Davey had done his job well. Lucy and Susan and Kent and Jonathan and Ted and Davey and a very small boy Mr. Newton had seen on the next block. Some were smiling, some were shy, and the little boy, Benjy, looked as if he might cry. But in a few minutes they had all been hugged and welcomed and Benjy was happily rocking on Mrs. Newton's lap.

Then there was another knock and nine more children stood on the porch.

"Goodness," said Mrs. Newton to her husband, "I'm glad we made that last batch of cookies."

Then two more came and four more and one more. Twenty-three children, of all possible sizes and shapes and colors and ages! It was more than they had dared to hope for, but there were enough cookies for everybody.

The ones who liked trucks and trains had trucks and trains to play with, and the ones who liked dolls had boy dolls and girl dolls. They played together with the doll house and the jigsaw puzzles and the Noah's Ark. They looked at the clock and listened to the cuckoo, and couldn't believe that Mr. Newton had made it all himself.

"He makes all sorts of things," said Mrs. Newton proudly.

"He fixed my trike," said Davey.

"Then—do you suppose you could take a look at my bike?" asked Susan. "The front wheel is acting funny."

Mr. Newton saw at once what was wrong and straightened it out, and showed Susan how to fix it if it happened again.

Mrs. Newton helped Lucy with her knitting and then showed them all how to make popcorn balls. Altogether they had a wonderful time.

Before the afternoon was over, Mrs. Newton had rocked more than thirty miles in her rocking chair, and Mr. Newton had told seventy different stories about how it was when he was a boy. Between them they had settled nine fierce arguments and seventeen smaller ones, and had bandaged endless scraped knees and elbows. They had even raised their voices to make themselves heard over the noise.

When the children left late in the afternoon, they promised to come back next Saturday.

The neat little house was a mess. Everything was topsy-turvy. The cuckoo called six times at five o'clock, and the clock was going tock-tick, tock-tick.

"Oh well," said Mrs. Newton, looking very pink and pleased, "we've got until next Saturday to get it straightened up. Are you sure there were enough toys and treats to go around?"

"There was enough of everything to go around," said Mr. Newton, giving his wife an enormous hug. "Toys and treats and LOVE!"